...It's a Panda Ining!

A visit to my world of Pathological Demand Avoidance

...for Leo and Ben...again.

All Rights Reserved ©2019 Rachel Jackson

A few opening words from Harry Thompson
– author of 'The PDA Paradox'

"When I was invited to review 'It's a PanDA thing', I felt honoured and delighted and accepted wholeheartedly.
It always fills my heart with joy whenever a new title is added to the ever-growing list of PDA literature – if there is one thing PDA is currently in dire need of, it's more recognition.

I often tell my own clients that the key to approaching, supporting and living with PDA lies not within a specific set of prescribed methods – but rather with building a deeper understanding of each individual PDAer's world such that your approach to their specific experience becomes second nature.

Although the story is written for children, it offers readers of all ages the first steps towards building that deeper understanding of Pathological Demand Avoidance – a very puzzling and little-understood part of the autism spectrum. With clear, delicate and fun use of language and charming and evocative illustrations, Rachel and Zeke have represented the multidimensional and at times harrowing nature of PDA as well as the many challenges the young PDA child faces – whilst still managing, with great finesse and a strong, unmissable overtone of optimism, to capture the more endearing sides of the condition – concluding on a positive note and delivering a brighter outlook to the reader.

As a PDAer myself I find that much of the time when I reflect on my childhood, I do so with unease. Each memory transports me back to a time when confusion, sadness and loneliness were, for the most part, all that I knew. Reading this story has helped me to reflect on my own journey – and I realise now that I have a choice as to how I view it: I can see it as an excruciating struggle...or as more of a 'scenic route', fraught with challenges to learn from that would also steer me towards the rich and fulfilling life I find myself in today.

Not only has Rachel's story offered the PDA child a clearer understanding of their own condition...but it also grants the adult PDAer like myself an opportunity to revisit their past with a new-found confidence and strength, thus rendering them more accepting of the turbulent past which constitutes who they are today."

Thank you Harry for your support and advice.
I'm sure this too is a beginning......

Authors note:

Last year I wrote a story...and then another one.
(If this book turns out to make no sense you might want to buy them ☺)

At the time I thought that was the end of it
...my little moment of authorship done.

I suppose I also thought we had arrived at a diagnosis
– and our journey through Autism and ASD had reached its destination.

I was wrong on both counts

There was another thing...

I knew Autism was a spectrum and had many flavours and colours,
I didn't know much about PDA.

It turns out neither did many other people.

This is my contribution to building the profile of this incredibly tough condition to live with and manage

and to helping myself to continue to learn, explore and love my way through it.

I hope you will continue to travel with me.

An introductory note on Pandas – with thanks to the PDA Society

Giant Pandas are highly sensitive creatures.
I'm not suggesting that they get offended easily….but that they can require very specific conditions and a carefully managed environment to enable them to thrive.

Children and adults with a presentation of Autism called Pathological Demand Avoidance – PDA – are very similar and also require an environment enriched with a set of well integrated support strategies.
It is for this reason that the PDA Society have adopted the Giant Panda as their ambassador. You can visit their website at https://www.pdasociety.org.uk for a huge amount of useful information on PDA.

The acronym PANDA also serves as a great way to remember helpful approaches with PDA:

P – Pick your battles
- minimise rules, provide choice and control and explain reasons

A – Anxiety Management
- Reduce uncertainty, recognise underlying anxiety and social/sensory challenges

N – Negotiation & Collaboration
- Keep calm, proactively collaborate and negotiate to solve problems

D – Disguise and Manage demands
- Manage perception of demands, balance with ability to tolerate

A – Adaptation
- Use humour, distraction & novelty and be flexible – always have a plan B !

They said I had a 'thing' they did...

....They called it ASD

...and then they came and changed their minds:

...it could be PDA

I don't care either way!

...I said...

It's all the same to me!

It's just the case that ASD has lots of different sorts

Some like to sit
and draw or read

....and some likes lots of sports.

Some kids are shy and really quiet...

...and others shout a lot.

.....and kids with PDA are quite an interesting lot..

The first thing you may notice
        if you came and spoke to me

...is that nothing's all that different –
        not that you would really see

I walk like you and talk like you

...play games and watch cartoons.

I laugh at jokes and tell tall tales...

...and like friends – just like you!

I like to ride my bike about...
...and climb and swing in trees.

I've always got a den somewhere...
And scabs upon my knees ☺

"So what is PDA?"

...you say – if you seem just like me?

Well maybe when it's time for tea you'd get a chance to see....

Cos when it comes to "turn off time" or that "we have to go..."

I may just freeze...

or run away...

Or I often just say **"NO!!"**

There's so much "NO" inside me that I want to scream and shout...

...I try to keep it all inside

...but often it gets out ☹

I know it's sometimes shocking
...and I know it might scare you

But when my brain's decided "No!"
there's not much I can do!

But not because of naughtiness...

I'm <u>not</u> horrible or mean

I just feel safe when *I'm* in charge – I <u>need</u> to make the rules

Which makes it hard to do what's asked

...especially when at school

It helps to get inventive
when I can't see <u>your</u> way round

.....I'll point out something interesting
or make a funny sound

I sometimes find the best way to avoid all life's demands

...is making up a rainbow

or pretending I'm a plant!

You'd be surprised if you could see how much I get upset...

...when I'm doing things that just don't work
...but can't stop doing yet

I worry lots and still I find I'm so misunderstood

If I *could* make different choices
then I really REALLY would!

PDA is tough sometimes for me and all my friends
My family help me all the time

....and my little brother Ben.

He often has to stay at home because I can't go out

He <u>must</u> get bored of playing spies...

....of that I have no doubt

I know you think I'm just a kid
 who won't do as he's told

Give me a chance

...and you will help my confidence unfold

I can be so creative
and have gifts you may not see

...just sometimes they feel locked away
and I can't find the key

We all have little some-things
that make us not the same

My PanDA thing is part of me
and really not to blame

I'm trying hard to be like you and learn to

I hope you'll like me even though

I often just say "No!"

From a parent (i.e. me):

I am just, as a parent, beginning to learn about PDA – in both a practical and theoretical sense.
This is my learning to share...yours is very likely to be different – as will mine on a different day ☺ – and so...

- PDA is inconsistent – one day is just one day. What works today may not tomorrow – let it go!

- Your child is not 'deliberately' defiant – although they may be consciously defy-ing. The aim is not to defy – but to retain control and the freedom to choose. That's not far off what we all want isn't it?

- PDA is a <u>part</u> of your child – an integral part – but not your <u>whole</u> child. Nourish who they are as a whole.

- Over time you will come to recognise the little things that you (or others) say that 'trip the switch'....

- ...and the things you can do or say to reset that switch and return to calm connectedness.

- In our house a cuddle works wonders...offered gently and at eye level....once the major flare subsides.

- The most crushing impact of a 'PDA explosion' is the immediate disconnect is causes between adult and child. The faster you can reconnect and reassure...the less anxiety and the faster the recovery.

- There are parts of PDA that are very different from a 'traditional' ASD profile – so don't let anyone tell you your child doesn't have ASD because 'he looked me in the eye' or 'she seems very sociable for an Aspie'
  ...PDA is a different flavour of ASD
  – but many of the 'classic' symptoms still underlie the PDA

  - PDA is <u>not</u> the same as ODD...or ADHD...but you'll have to look them all up to understand why ☺

Advice I have 'stolen' (from experts – who know a lot more than me ☺)

- Children with PDA need to be able to say 'No'. – they need to feel like they have a choice (we all do really)

- If you can't give ultimate control – emphasise the parts that they can control – "We will be going to Grandmas' today – you can choose what you would like to take with you"

- Avoid using 'demand words such as need / must / will or won't / can't / now and also deadlines and ultimatums – they cause greater anxiety and reduce clear thinking and action

- Allow additional processing time – your request takes longer to navigate through the anxiety it caused

- Focus on requests – often more creative language works well – "Would you be so kind as to…"

- Engage the creativity and humour of your child when they are 'stuck' – they are in fight/flight mode (sympathetic nervous system) and you can help them to activate the parasympathetic system responsible for diffusing panic – music, drawing, Lego can all help to rebalance and regain rational thinking

- Allow them to take the initiative in making others happy by offering vague hints and loose suggestions

- Share responsibility – "I'll do that and you could do this and that way we can do it together"

- If your child doesn't enjoy compliments, share your opinion on their actions and outcomes rather than praising identity and personal characteristics that they can't control

- Lastly – but most importantly – pick your battles! Trust and connection beat battling every time ☺

About the Author:

Rachel studied Psychology at Royal Holloway University of London before training in counselling, coaching and NLP. She worked for 6 years in London as management consultant and went self employed in 2007 with a view to shifting her own work-life balance.

Whilst travelling independently around South East Asia she met her South African partner, Brad and they settled where Rachel grew up in rural Suffolk.

Rachel is now the mother of two boys - Leo (8½) and Ben (6¾). She balances her own coaching, facilitation and leadership development company - Changing Dialogues Ltd with the challenges of bringing up a family.

Leo was diagnosed in 2015 with High Functioning Asperger's. At risk of exclusion from successive local primary schools he has been welcomed for over two years in a fabulous Pupil Referral Unit near his home.
Now taking daily taxi-treks to attend school in Cambridge...it has been here that the words Pathological Demand Avoidance have first been uttered. This journey is simply a continuation of what will be a long evolution.

Rachel dedicates this book once again with love to all the incredible friends, family, teachers, support workers and complete strangers who have helped both her and her family on this extraordinary journey.

Rachel...has her own thing!

Find out more about Rachel's 'day-job' at www.changingdialogues.com

About the Illustrator:

Zeke Clough is an illustrator based in Todmorden, best known...so far...for his distinctive sleeve artwork for electronic musicians such as Shackleton and Ekoplekz. His partner of eight years has 14 year old autistic twins who go to a specialist communication school.

Zeke's love of comic strips and drawing has proved to be an effective way to communicate with the boys. When they were younger their favourite toys were included in the comics – they either give advice or learned along with the boys. Many a meltdown or hazardous situation was circumvented by a quickly drawn explanatory comic strip!

Zeke also works for a mental health charity supporting school children to develop an understanding of the importance of good mental health and providing them with a language to discuss these issues. His illustrations also support his work with refugees/asylum seekers and adults with mental health difficulties.

In recent years, Zeke has been commissioned to support delegates at a number of neurodiversity conferences –drawing graphic notes to recall their learning effectively.

In the future he hopes to publish his social stories more widely, and to continue to explore mental health and autism related issues through comic strips and animation.

Zeke too has his things.

see more of Zeke's work at www.zekeclough.co.uk

Lightning Source UK Ltd.
Milton Keynes UK
UKHW022132160621
385638UK00006B/57